SOUTHERN SHORTS

SUE MYDLIAK

Copyright © 2018 by Sue Mydliak

Layout design and Copyright © 2024 by Next Chapter

Published 2024 by Next Chapter

Edited by Graham (Fading Street Services)

Cover art by Jaylord Bonnit

This book is a work of fiction. Names, characters, places, and incidents are the product of the author's imagination or are used fictitiously. Any resemblance to actual events, locales, or persons, living or dead, is purely coincidental.

All rights reserved. No part of this book may be reproduced or transmitted in any form or by any means, electronic or mechanical, including photocopying, recording, or by any information storage and retrieval system, without the author's permission.

I dedicate this book to Tom Hernandez. He was my biggest fan of these stories.

ACKNOWLEDGMENTS

I'd like to thank my writing family for their patience as I finally got all these stories put together into a collection the best Southern Shorts I have. They have shown such a love for them, and it's been such a pleasure to write them and read them as well. So, to my WriteOn Joliet family, and especially to Tom to who I dedicate this book to. I give you my first collection of Southern Shorts.

CONTENTS

Foreword — vi

1. Blender Fiasco — 1
2. Poo-Pourri — 6
3. Got Your Back Jack — 11
4. Punking Southern Style — 17
5. Flip-Flop Catastrophe — 23
6. Some Like It Hot — 27
7. Red Apple Cataclysm — 35
8. Beach Party Zombie — 41
9. Love On The Fly — 47
10. Shredded Wheat Catastrophe — 52
11. Winter's Rally — 59
12. Santa's Got A Brand-New Bag — 63

About the Author — 68

"Welcome! My name is Charlese and I'll be your waitress today at the Chubbie Wieners. Come sit down and let me get you a cup of coffee. We have to talk. Now, I don't normally sit down with the customers, but I can tell that you and I are going to be real good friends. Yeah, I can! You have such a pleasant smile and all and...Chester! Get Eleanor out here to do tables, I'm busy with a customer. Thank you! Now where was I? Oh, I remember, you and I becoming friends. That's right! Well, let me tell you about our little town. You're new here, right? Thought so. So, let me be the Ambassador of Dry Prong and give you our little tale on how we came to be. Need a warm up on your coffee? No? Alright then.

Dry Prong was incorporated as a village in 1945.

According to tradition, the village received its name when a family moved to the region in the 1870s to build a sawmill. To power the mill, they built a water wheel, only to discover that the creek over which they had built it went dry every summer: the creek was a "dry prong". The mill was soon rebuilt over a nearby creek which flowed all year, but the name stuck. The creek is now outside the city limits, on Highway 123. Shane Davis is the current mayor of the village." (**https://en.wikipedia.org/wiki/Dry_Prong,_Louisiana**)

1

BLENDER FIASCO

"No one, and I mean one, knows how to create madness and mass hysteria better than my neighbor Willodean. In this story, Willodean is fighting for her life over a fruit smoothie. So, sit down, take a load off your feet, and be prepared for a pretty fascinating story!"

I awoke to screams, coming from my neighbor's house.
Quickly, I grabbed my robe and sprinted outside. By the time I reached my neighbor's front door, my pink bunny slippers, once perky, looked like drowned rats ... dew was their undoing.

The screaming persisted.

"Willodean? You alright?"

No answer. *Can she hear me?*

Usually, the door is locked, but at this point I didn't give a rat's ass and gave the door a wild kick. Down it went and in I went!

There stood Willodean in shock, sporting food from head to toe. From where I stood you could see all the way into the kitchen, bungalows are great that way and that's where I found her, between the kitchen and the dining room.

"You kicked my door down! What the hell, Charlese?"

She was furious with me ... the one who came to her aid. "You were screaming, and you woke me up. That's how loud you were!"

"But you kicked my damn door down! Why would you do that?"

Granted, I didn't check to see otherwise, but when your neighbor, your *friend*, is screaming bloody murder, you don't do polite things. You go in for the kill.

"You sounded like you were being killed, so I've come to save your butt!"

"But you kicked down my door!" Willodean hadn't moved from her spot upon my arrival, and it was probably due to the fact that she had so much food, juice and whatever else on her that she became *glued* to the floor.

"Ok, can we just get past that part for now?" I told her. "You ok? You look a mess." She did too: hair all tousled about as if a hurricane had gone through it and body all covered with food and juice. If I didn't know any better, I'd say she was in a food fight.

She waved her hand aimlessly about, with a confused look on her face, as though she didn't know what had happened. 'Dazed' would be the perfect word to describe her.

"I, I ..." She motioned toward the blender, "It attacked me."

Ok. That was ... *different*. I snorted and grabbed my abdomen in a fit of laughter.

"Charlese, it's not funny, it really did. I had to protect myself!" She was pleading for her life, but it looked more like a drowned kitten meowing to be fluffed up dry.

That made me laugh even harder.

"Oh, Willodean, you can't be serious! What'd it do? Try to blend you?" My words were barely audible because I was laughing so hard.

"Why, yes, yes it did," she said proud and indignant.

Grabbing onto the counter for support, I slowly sank to the floor, convulsing with laughter, and clutching my side. My insides hurt so badly that I thought they would explode.

She just stood there, messy and annoyed. After a few minutes had gone by, I had composed myself as best as I could, but it was hard. Just one look at her sorrowful face ... I, no I didn't have the heart. She truly needed some words of comfort, and I was going to do just that.

"Now, hunny, blenders don't attack people," I said.

She pointed to the blender again as if to say, *yes, they do!* But I knew better. I would try to get her to see reason, which, for Willodean, would be no easy task.

"No, no they don't sweetie," I said. "You may have gotten a spoon stuck in it, but it did not attack you."

"Charlese, you're never to put a spoon in a blender when it's running. That's just common sense!"

This is a girl who just claimed a blender had attacked her, and she's telling me about common sense. *Right.*

After a calming breath, I said, "Willodean, sit down before you have another episode. You're a bit confused, not to mention scary at the moment."

I took a deep breath. "Tell me what is going on; how'd the mean ol' blender *attack* you?"

"Stop treating me like an infant, Charlese. I know what I saw. I was making a smoothie for breakfast, you know the one with strawberries and bananas, when it sucked my hand down inside. The thing was ready to chop me up into tiny pieces." Willodean's emotions were at an all-time high. When she gets frustrated, fight or flight mode kicks in and it's usually the flight mode she resembles.

I needed a moment of silence to register what I just heard, but then Willodean emotions fired up again.

"I ... I had to defend myself," Willodean continued, her voice shaky. "It was like the blender had taken hold of my very hand." She waved her digits in front of my face, her way of being dramatic. "So, I started to punch at it and when that didn't work, I unplugged it, but it kept on going! It was like something out of the Twilight Zone, Charlese!"

"I see." I have to admit, I was interested, a little weirded out, but as her friend, I had to go along with her. "So, let me get this straight: all you did was make a smoothie and the blender went all crazy on you?"

"Yup."

I walked over to the blender that now lay on its side; bits of strawberries and banana, not to mention juice, were all over the counter and floor. I looked at the blender, and thought about it for a moment, a long moment. Willodean now had me spooked about this appliance. I shook my head. I was being stupid. Cautiously I went to upright the blender, and it turned on me.

Willodean let out a loud scream, grabbed me from behind and pulled.

It was too late. The monster had me already. The whirl of the blades sucked my hand closer and closer. My life flashed before my eyes: Chester, Chubby Weiner, and my Gran. This would make an epic movie.

All the while, we struggled against the dang thing, and we might have been defeated if not for Willodean. When she couldn't pry it off my hand, she ran for the garage and got the blow torch.

"Willodean, my hand is in this thing," I hollered frantically. "You're gonna melt it over my hand!" Now, I would've trusted anyone else to do this, but not Willodean. Trusting Willodean to do anything that was remotely dangerous was like jumping off a cliff thinking you could fly.

"I know what I'm doing, trust me," she assured me. When I torch it, you fling it off your hand as hard as you can. You got that?"

I shook my head but said, "Yeah."

"One, two ... three!"

When she torched the blender, I flung the thing as hard as I could, only it connected with Willodean's head. Down she went for the count and out the window went the smoldering kitchen appliance, truly a sight to behold. Willodean, on the other hand, was a heap of girl: food and a welt as big as a golf ball forming on her forehead. *Ouch.*

Days have passed since that horrific morning. We don't talk much about it. In fact, we don't say a word. Willodean has no use for blenders anymore. Can't say that I blame her.

2

POO-POURRI

"People never cease to amaze me, especially with the products they come up with. Very inventive I must say. It just so happened, when I was working my shift at the Chubbie Wieners, an opportunity made its way to me, and it was a 'stinker'."

Aljonette Breland, now there's a name that's not hard to forget, nor is the person it's attached to.

Aljonette came to us this past summer. It was June, and the hottest day of the year too. I was working at the Chubbie Weiners when she stepped in and sat at one of my booths.

Like all newcomers, she had an air about her that stuck out like a pimple. She walked in, nose up, and just as prim and proper as a lady could be and then some. As for her attire, I'd say it went well with her personality ... tight.

"Harlon, stuff your eyeballs back into your head before

your wife does ... shame on you!" I said. He gave me a sorrowful look, and went back to eating.

I then, in turn, walked over to where she sat down, and gave her my most cheerful howdy and asked if I could get her a drink and menu. What happened next blew me away.

Her head turned slowly toward me, and said, "What's that clone you have on hunny?"

"Clone? Oh, you mean, cologne! Um, Ode de Hamburger." I thought it was funny, she didn't.

"I see. I'd like a glass of whutur if'n you don't mind?"

"Of course. Be right back."

Whoa and double whoa. What planet did she come from? I took a clean glass from the shelf, scooped some ice and filled it full of H2o. My eyes never left hers. She was something else. Just what that was, I'm not sure.

"Who is she Charlese? She's kinda pretty don't you think?"

Raylene, is our newest waitress to the Chubbie Weiner, sweet, young, and not a lot of brains, but the customers sure like her, especially the men. Raylene likes brightly colored clothes and tight tops. God gave her a rack that didn't quit. Oh, I'm not jealous ... much, but when she leans over the tables, the customers get an eyeful.

"Pretty? Raylene, if her clothes got any tighter, I swear you'd have to roll her out of here. Besides, I don't know how she can walk, let alone sit in that booth. I'm afraid her clothes are gonna split at the seams!" I looked around the joint, and sure enough, all the men were waiting for that same thing to happen.

I walked away in disgust with her glass of water in hand and set it on the table.

"Will there be anything else?"

Again, her head turned slowly. It was like watching the Exorcist.

"Jewant to sit a moment? Ah've got some fahn clone to show ya."

I usually don't sit at the customer's tables, but for some odd reason, I did!

She took out this bottle and set it on the table before me ... Poopourri. Oh, my lord, poo scented potpourri! Eww!

"I don't mean to be disrespectful, but I ain't going to spray feces on any part of me, thank you."

She started in to giggle, and said, "This ain't poop deah! It's clone!" And sprayed some on her wrist.

"Ah's don't sprays it on mae, it's fowa the toilet! Whuns yew done! Smale!"

I hesitated, but she sprayed some in the air and it smelled like Peonies. "You mean, whenyou're done with ... your business, you spray the toilet?"

She nodded her head.

"Oh, why, that's kinda clever! We shore, I mean, sure could use something like that in the restrooms here! How much?"

"Nuhn duhlars."

"Ok, I'll buy two! I'll be right back."

Chester was in his office when I came rushing in.

"What's wrong? Some guy pinching your butt again? Because if they are ... ?"

"No! I just came in her to get my purse."

"You leaving? Your shift isn't over yet."

Men can be so annoying sometimes. "If you must know, I'm buying the restaurant some potpourri for the restrooms."

"Oh Charlese, I wish you wouldn't ... "

Too late, I had already left and was back at her booth.

"Here is my eighteen dollars, Thanks so much! By the way, you're new here, what's your name?"

"Aljonette Breland."

"Well, it's nice to meet you Aljonette, hope to see you again soon!"

With that she gave me a smile, stood up and walked out the door the same way she came in ... slow.

A week had gone by, I hadn't seen Aljonette, but my good friend and neighbor, Willodean, had come back from vacation and stopped by the CHubbie Weiners for a bite.

"Hey, I see you're back! How was your vacation?" I said, as I wiped down the counter at the bar.

"Oh, Charlese, it was wonderful! I saw so many things and all the stores were so cute. In fact, I purchased something for you, I hope you like it. I thought it to be very clever." She held out a bright, pink bag, with tissue paper sticking out of the top.

"You didn't have to get me anything, Willodean, but thank you for thinking of me just the same!"

I pulled the tissues out very carefully and inside was a bottle of Poopourri.

"Oh, I just bought myself a bottle of this stuff from a new customer. Her name, um, oh, Aljonette Breland!"

"My cousin! She was here?"

Red flags and bells started to ring and wave in my head just then. This can't be good. Really, it can't.

"Your cousin, really? Why shut my mouth..." nervously tittering, "small world huh?"

"Well, I'll have to look hur up. She said she'd drop on by for a spell. Take a whiff, you'll like it! Bought it off of some old lady at some craft show. Have to say, I felt sorry for her."

"Why?"

"No one was buying her stuff!"

RED FLAGS! RED FLAGS!

If I had learned anything with Willodean, it's not to trust her. She's a sweetheart, don't get me wrong, but her heart can sometimes be misplaced if you know what I mean. That, and, the bus doesn't always stop where she gets off either. Brian fart in other words.

Cautiously, I held the bottle in my hand, while my other moved to remove its top. I guess moving too slow had Willodean on edge, so she grabbed it and gave me a full spray.

"Oh, my lord! Why, that smells like shit!" she screamed.

I just withered in my spot.

3

GOT YOUR BACK JACK

"Magic, when done right has such an amazing effect on those of us who are to blind to see that it is just an act. Nothing real. To others though, it's like Harry Potter had invaded our little neck of the woods and we're all agog. In this next story, Willodean and I have a bit of trouble. Let's see how we do."

Summer had come with a vengeance. I woke in the morning with the sheets clinging to my legs.

"Great."

Normally I love summer, but when it gets hotter than a pancake grilling on the pan, I just melt. I was sitting at my table, drinking my morning coffee, and reading the newspaper, when someone knocked on my back door. Peeking around the corner, I saw that it was my neighbor Willodean Ferris.

"Hey, girl, what brings you here this hot morning? Come on in, can I get you anything to drink?"

Willodean was my closest and dearest friend. Her hair was strawberry blonde, and she had blue eyes and a body that was pleasing to the eye. She was a beaut. My brother, Dean, always wanted to go out with her, but being the chicken that he was, he'd drool from a distance and dream away. I can only imagine what those dreams were like, but that would be a little bit disgusting, not to mention creepy.

"If you got lemonade, I'd love some. If not, I'll be just fine. Parched, but fine, nevertheless." She sat down just as neat as a pin with her cut-off shorts and a pink tank top and ... bare feet?

I had some lemonade, pink, and handed her a glass.

"Willodean, where are your sandals, or any shoes for that matter?" This really struck a chord with me, because Willodean is the Queen of fashion, the girl who thinks that feet without shoes are naked.

"Oh my God, Willodean, you're naked! You're never naked!"

"Charlese, stop! I know this is so out of the norm for me, but I had to rush right over and show you ... um, you have sandals I could borrow for a smidge?"

I looked at her quizzically. "Ah, ya sure, hang on a sec."

I ran and got my shocking, hot pink flip-flops with rhinestones and brought them out to her. "They're a mite big for you, so if ..."

"Hush, I'm not going anywhere with your sandals, just gonna use them."

She placed them on the floor in front of her and stared at them. I mean, *really* stared at them. It was an odd moment for us. I wasn't sure if I should sit next to her and stare along, or say a prayer, although I don't think she was praying 'cause her eyes were open and all.

"Willodean? What are you doing, hunny?" I whispered.

"Shhhh," Her eyes never looked at me, she just kept on staring. Damn if this wasn't boring.

There we sat, like two peas in a pod, staring at my shocking, hot pink flip-flops with rhinestones, could we get more stranger than that? After about five minutes had passed, I was starting to get sleepy, and then it happened, one of the sandals moved.

"Oh. my gosh, how did you do that?" I yelled.

"It's called telekinesis; I've been practicing every night."

"Well, what for? I mean, it's cool and all, but does it have a purpose?" It was a neat trick.

"Well, it would come in handy if I'm attacked, especially if the weapon is not in reach."

Poor thing was dead serious. Got to hand it to her though, Willodean was always thinking of ways of protecting herself. I admired that.

"Hunny, if it took you this long to make one sandal move a centimeter, you best call the undertaker first."

"Charlese, aren't you the tiniest bit excited about this?" She was truly hurt.

"Oh, I am, but I'm looking at it realistically too. If you want to really protect yourself, you need to start locking your doors, because you don't. This little trick of yours is all that it is a trick; cool one at that, but nothing more."

I got up and started to wash the few dishes I had in the sink. Willodean was down in the dumps and got up to leave.

"Well, I guess I'll go. Thanks for ... well, thanks." The door creaked and slammed shut before I could get a word in edgewise. Put an apology on my list of 'to do's'. I heaved a heavy sigh.

I was about to go outside and do some gardening when I thought I saw a man. He was lurking in the backyard. I checked again, and sure enough, there he was. He just stood there, looking at me. Creepy. I kept my eyes glued to him until he vanished into thin air, right before my eyes.

"Whoa, now that was incredible and a mite scary at that." I wandered outside and had myself a look about. I scoured the backyard, the sides, and the front, but he wasn't in sight. As I turned to go toward the backyard, he was right in front of me, tall, dark and ... really creepy, but in a good way. Have you ever read those stories about meeting a tall, dark, and handsome man? Well, this was him. He wore dark pants, shoes, shirt and had dark eyes. His hair was dark too. This man was dark all over, and lord if I didn't want to jump his bones, but I composed myself and tried to look frightened in a sexy way, which probably didn't come across as that. More like a bee had stung me.

"Haven't you ever heard of approaching people without showing up completely by surprise and right in front of them? Haven't you ever heard of personal space?" And motioned the area around me so that he understood what I was talking about. Didn't help.

"Personal space? What is this personal space?" His voice was soft, like butter, and it glided so smoothly into my ear. I wished I was toasted bread just then.

I saw my hula-hoop and fetched it, placing it on the ground next to him.

"Step in." I pointed.

"Why? Are you imprisoning me?" His face was so fine, something right out of Renaissance time. He was sure pretty.

I snorted. He's dumber than a box of rocks.

"It's a hula-hoop! You know, you put it around your waist and wiggle your hips." He seemed to like that idea.

"I like hips. I like your hips." He got this look about him that led me to believe that he had more than hula-hooping going on.

Ok, now he was creepy again.

"You want to know about personal space, or don't you?" I was truly annoyed.

"Actually, I came by to visit you. You are so ... so beautiful, so breathtaking, that I had to see you. Make love to me."

Well, that's a fine howdy-do if you ask me. As much as I would love to accept his invitation to jump his bones, I thought it might be a bit on the fast side, seeing how I didn't even know his name.

"Hunny, as much as I would love to accept your so-called invitation, I don't think that would be a good idea." I wondered what he looked like without his clothes. I bet he's got a six pack under that shirt, and I can't begin to image what's in his pants, but I have a pretty good idea. I grinned.

"Why not? Am I not presentable enough for you?" He held his arms out to the sides and rotated around.

He displayed himself very nicely, and I have to admit, I wanted to change my mind, but I didn't.

"Oh, you're hunky enough, that's for sure, but you're also a bit creepy. Sorry, don't mean to be rude." I started for my door when I found myself in the clutches of his strong, masculine arms.

"I want you and I will...kiss me." He leaned his head down just as I was about to scream, then something hit me in the head, a pink flip flop with rhinestones; my sandal!

Who in the hell is throwing my shoes at my head? I thought.

"You let her go, you, you monster, you!"

Well, what do you know, it's my knight in shining armor, Willodean, and she's come to save me ... with sandals. How courageous of her.

My monster of a man let me fall to the ground and I scooted back. He looked at Willodean, then me, then back to her and smiled. Oh, this wasn't good. It was Willodean's turn to have a go with Mr. Hunkiness. Willodean, upon seeing his intentions, stared at the nearest weapon ... the hose. Oh, good lord, this was not going to turn out in her favor, his yes, hers ... no. She stared with all her might and she gave it a real good try. Her eyes got all serious and sweat beaded off her head, when all of a sudden, the hose started to wiggle and then, it spurted out some water. That was it. Yay for the bit of grass that got some water. Next thing you know, Better Homes and Gardens will be coming out to take a picture of my lawn.

"Willodean, did ya ..." Nope, she didn't.

I was not going to have my day ruined by some man who couldn't take no for an answer. I saw my Granddaddy's ax up against the tool shed and I stared. Then, I thought to hell with that, and went to pick it up. As soon as I did, I marched over to him and connected right into Mr. Hunkiness's head, and down he went. Willodean looked at me with total awe.

"Charlese, you did it!"

"Willodean, people say, *practice makes perfect*, but my Gran always told me to practice is a waste of time, just do it, so I did! You want some more lemonade?"

4

PUNKING SOUTHERN STYLE

"Chester Bertie, now he's one terrific guy. Very creative also! Steampunk had made its run in Dry Prong for a while, and it made quite an impression on the kids around here. I've seen some crazy getups, but the one getup I couldn't be prouder of was what Chester had made. To this day, I have no idea what it was called, only that it made quite an impression on our 'Lady of the Evening.'"

Have you ever wondered what it would be like to see someone achieve greatness? I have, and it was ... great.

I live in Dry Prong, Louisiana and have all my life. No one I know gets the newspaper because our population is about 421, at least that's what it was back in 2000, and I can't imagine that it's gotten any higher than that. You see, when you live in a town that small, everyone knows what everyone's up too. Gosh, keeping secrets around here is like trying to keep Herbert's cows from straying off the pasture and into Mrs. Laradell's garden, lord have mercy! It just can't be done!

Anyway, Chester Bertie is my boss at Chubby Wieners, and even though Chester has no college degree, he is smarter than a bullwhip. The things he comes up with just blows my mind and I have to think, there's a story to be told there. Chester and I go a long way. I've been working for him for ten years now and there have been times where our friendship has been, well, let's just say we have benefits, not the work kind either.

One day I came in early because I had some things to do before my shift began. I was putting my purse away in my locker when Chester came in.

"Hey Charlese, I was wondering if you could stop by after work, I've got something to show ya."

I turned to look at him, all tired like. "Oh Chester, not tonight, I'm really not up to it. I haven't been sleeping very ..."

"Oh, it's nothing like that! Shoot, if I wanted you to see my, well, you know, I would have just come out with it! No, I created something that's really cool and I wanted your opinion. So, would you?"

He seemed scared and bashful, which wasn't Chester at all. Lord, the man was an animal in bed, so this was surprising to me.

"Why, sure Chester, I'd be glad to see what you made!" And I smiled at him as I went out into the restaurant to get things set up for my shift.

Thank goodness the night went fast. The usual crowd came in, you know the kind, the boisterous men who'd come in after work and get a pitcher of beer and try to pinch my rear. I swear the next one who tries isn't going to be standing straight, nor is his voice gonna sound husky. Then there's Pansy Crumpler, the town's 'lady of the Evening'. She always comes in around six-ish, looking like someone tried to put a square peg into a cylinder and call it *sexy*, and I don't know who told her that red lipstick looks great against yellow teeth, but it really doesn't.

"Hey Charlese, how about my usual?" She parked her big red caboose at the bar stool and placed a cigarette between her two fingers, holding it there. I just rolled my eyes and shook my head. She does this every night, expecting some pitiful bystander, namely a man, to light it for her, but as usual, no one did. They know too much about her – that, and they all want children someday. I don't blame them for staying away, but I have to give her credit, she does try.

"Hey Pansy, you need a light?" Chester, always the man to come to her aid.

"Well, I ain't holding it for my health now, am I?"

"Um no but smoking them things ain't for your health either." He took out his lighter, lit the cigarette, and got back to work.

I got her *usual* which was water with a lemon twist. Ain't she the exciting type?

"Is there anything else I can get you?" I kept my voice as perky as I could get without showing my annoyance. Gran always told me that a person can go a long way with politeness, and she was usually right.

Pansy looked at me as if I were a fly ready to be swatted.

"Do I look like I need anything else?" She blew her cigarette smoke in my face and turned to face the other way.

Well, I could come up with a hundred things that she could need, like personality for one. Damn, my apple tree has more personality than she does. I swiftly turned on my heels and walked away. One of these days, just one, I'd like to take her cigarettes and do something wicked to them.

Finally, at midnight, the restaurant closed, and Chester and I locked up for the night. He only lived down the block from the restaurant, so we walked it. It was a beautiful night. The moon was out, and the frogs were singing their love songs to one another. I wondered what they were saying. We arrived and he led me to his garage in the back. Chester had an enormous garage, two car, but he didn't have a vehicle, so it was his workshop.

"Ok, now, I don't want you to laugh when you see it, ok?" His hand was on the doorknob and I could see he was tense.

"Chester, I wouldn't do that to you. Come on now, show me what you got!" I put some emphasis on the *show me what you got* line, and he smiled right back. He has the whitest teeth.

He opened the door a tiny bit, stuck his hand in and turned on the light. This was getting exciting. Then, he opened it fully and motioned for me to enter and I did. There it was, it was huge and ... and ... I'm not quite sure how to explain it. It looked like a dinosaur with armor. It had so many rivets, dials, and thingamajigs on it, I wasn't sure if I should say, "Oh great!" or in a scary tone, "Oh ... great."

"Chester, this is, this is really great ... what is it?" As I slowly made my rounds, eyeing it up and down, but not touching it. Nope, that I would not do. Darn thing might come alive and then I'd have to scream.

"Shoot Charlese, this here is, well, it's my Tyransmafoghicle; it takes me where I need to go." Then his smile got big as a Cheshire Cat.

I just looked at him, admired his innovation, and then got dead serious.

"Chester, you go anywhere, and I mean *anywhere* with this thing and you're gonna scare the living daylights out of everyone. Why, if you came across Mrs. Dewanna on her way to the Ladies Auxiliary driving that thing, she'd drop dead right on the spot. You know she has a condition, not to mention the police and Jermane Bumfree, he's our deputy, has been itching to haul someone in."

Jermane Bumfree was our man of the hour on the police force, always doing his job even when it didn't call for it, and nine times out of ten they didn't call for it. Then it hit me.

"Chester, I do believe it has a purpose."

The restaurant was busier than a beehive when, right on the money, Pansy Crumpler came walking in. She was all dolled up in a bright green, skin-tight skirt that would make a sausage wince, a black, low cut top that showed way too much for my liking, and pumps, those where the only thing on her that I thought was cute, in a slutty way, but cute nevertheless. I tried to maintain composure, but I had been waiting for this night for a long, long time. My *just dessert* was about to be had.

"Well, hello Pansy, can I get you your usual?" I purposely made sure I was extra perky, annoyingly so, and it worked.

"What do you think? Do I have to spell it out to you every time I come in this dump?" She crossed her leg, or tried, the darn thing was heavier than a cheesecake sliced thin.

"Why, of course not silly, I'll be back in a jiffy." That was my cue.

Now, Pansy had a pink Cadillac because she was a Mary Kay consultant, although I don't know, usually that stuff works really well on other people, but on her, it just messed her up something awful. As I was saying, she has this car and parks it right under the streetlight in front of our restaurant, which was perfect, because I had a plan.

"Pansy! Come quick, someone hit your car and sped off. I couldn't get the license plate number though!" Then I went back outside ... and waited.

"What?" She came charging out the front door and came face to face with 'Mr. Tyransmafoghicle'. His mouth was wide open as steam poured out and all them thingamajigs twinkling like stars. It was horrific, and Pansy was the star of the show. She screamed so loud that everyone that was in the restaurant came out to see and they got a load full. There she was, arms up as if she were up against a wall, mouth gaping, eyes bugging, and water in a puddle around her feet, she wet herself, then fainted.

"Show's over, time to go back in folks, beer is on the house!"

We all hooped and hollered our praises, and no one bothered Pansy, she just lay there like a dead skunk on the road. It was a sight to behold.

Chester got out of his vehicle, stepped over Pansy, and into his establishment, where he cranked out beer all night long. The one other thing that made this night memorable, other than scaring the bejeezus out of Pansy, was the fun I had with Chester in the 'Tyransmafoghicle'. It was a tad cramped inside, but we made it work out just fine.

5

FLIP-FLOP CATASTROPHE

"Summer in Dry Prong can get mighty hot and like all sandals are a must. For some it's not a big deal. Just put em' on and off you go! Others, well, it's like learning how to walk all over again. Seriously. This story is about my good friend and neighbor, Willodean. She decided to deal with the 'devil'."

Have you ever wondered why they call flip-flops, flip-flops? Because the damn things are nearly impossible to walk in! Take my friend Willodean for instance, she is the guru of fashion here in Dry Prong. Why the Lady Auxiliary follows her blog as to how one should dress! Lord, if you don't know how to dress yourself by now, then that's just a pity, but they swear by her. I just shudder.

One Saturday, I was outside, attending to my vegetable garden. Now, I'm not one of those who wears shorts, a tank top and jewelry to go yanking up weeds. I am more sensible than that. I wore my overalls, with a white, short-sleeved T-shirt, and work boots. Gloves of course. Don't want to mess my manicure.

So, like I said, I was outside. The sun blazed away and sweat trickled down my back when I heard a funny sound. I looked up ... sure enough it was Willodean, walking ... well, I'm not quite sure if you'd call it that. She reminded me of a dog, whose owner put them little boots on their paws. I don't even know why they do that. Poor little thing. They've got to be traumatized by it! I mean, have you ever seen them walk? It's pure torture! Funny ... but torture! Aside from the weird walk, she was dressed to the hilt.

"What in ... what's wrong with your feet? You put polish on and didn't wait for them to dry? If I told you once, I've told you a thousand times, you have to wait before walking anywhere!"

"No, I'm wearing flip-flops. Not quite sure how to keep them from falling off though! There weren't any instructions! Can you imagine that?"

"I can imagine you thinking that way."

"What did you say?"

"Ah, nothing."

I closed my eyes. Someone dropped her at birth. Couldn't be anything else. It would explain a whole lot.

"Willodean, just walk!"

"I am!"

"No, you're not! I don't know what you would call it, but it ain't walking that's for sure."

"But they keep falling off! See!" And she demonstrated for me. They fell off.

Annoyed, I stomped out of my garden, sat on the ground, and undid my boots.

"Give me."

"Give you what?"

"Give me those sandals."

"They're not sandals, they're flip-flops."

I gave her my death stare and said, "I don't give a damn what they're called. Call them waffles for all I care, just give them to me ... now!"

She sat next to me and handed them over.

"Now, watch." I commanded.

I walked away from her, turned, and then came back. "Now, you try. Walk the same way I did, which is walking."

I watched with much trepidation, as she placed them on her feet. She got up and started to march. Again.

"Willodean, just walk. Just. Walk. Pretend you have regular shoes on."

"But I don't have regular shoes on. I have flip-flops on my feet!"

"WALK!"

She froze. I guess she turned her brain on, because when she tried again, her walk was different. Yeah, that it was. More like she was on stilts. It was pathetic, just — I don't know how to explain it, but it was bad. I sighed.

Questions like "How?" and "Why?" cropped in my head.

"Willodean, answer me this? Did you never, ever wear flip-flops when you were little?"

"No. Mama said they were evil."

Should I ask?

A voice coming off my right shoulder said, "RUN!" While another voice on my left side said, "GO FOR IT!"

I tried hard, real hard to keep from doing what I knew would be a HUGE mistake, but I had to know. Why? Stumps me every time.

In a calm, but clearly, irritated voice I asked, "How?"

She was unbelievable.

"They're the spawn of the devil."

"Then, why are you wearing them if they are the spawn of the devil?"

I must love torture because I keep asking for it.

"Well, everyone wears them. Even you, Charlese! And you're not evil. So, I figured they had to be a tall tale my mama made up."

"But can I ask how? Or better yet, why?" I held the last word out longer, putting my emphasis on it, as a way to show great irritation.

"Oh, well, you see the thingy you put between your toes? And the two straps that come on either side of your foot?"

"Yeah ..."

"It looks forked. Like a serpent's tongue. You see the snake, Adam and Eve and all. See evil."

There was a long pause before I put my boots back on, grabbed the hose and blasted her with it.

"Oh, I'm sorry! The devil made me do it."

6

SOME LIKE IT HOT

"As summer continues, so does one's imagination. I think the heat does something to our brains, because what happened here one summer's night was pure fantasy. It all started at the Chubbie Wieners, toward the end of my shift and it was a hot one. I know for one thing if I ever get heat exhaustion again, I'd like it to be exactly how I had it that night."

In Dry Prong, Louisiana, it's hot and with the heat comes mean, ornery people. People who are normally nice you know, but on a day like today, they'd rip your head off.

I was working at the Chubby Weiner one night and sweat was dripping off me like butter drips off corn on the cob. I was in no mood to have anyone else tell me what was wrong with their food, let alone take on someone's suggestive remarks ... pigs.

I was listening, just waiting for someone to blurt something foul my way and then I'd let them have it. To make sure that wouldn't happen, I glared my intentions as I walked past them. I know that I shouldn't be doing that, especially if I wanted tips, but I didn't care. All I wanted to do was get home and take a cold shower, and then it happened. He waltzed in.

Oh, he was fine. He was tall, not too muscular, but just enough to start the drools a drooling and lord if his pants didn't fit him just right and to top it all off, he wore no shirt. I thought I'd cry.

I kept my eyes on him like a Hound Dog watching a Pheasant. I needed to see where he was gonna sit and in doing so, he saw me looking. Good. Then he pointed to the booth by the door, I shook my head no, then he pointed to another booth which still wasn't in my area, again, no. I looked like I was doing my neck exercises in the middle of the restaurant.

Ruby who caught sight of me, looked to see where I was staring, that's when her mouth dropped open. I wanted to tell her she looked like a cod fish, but then she started reeling for him. *Oh, no you don't Ruby, I saw him first dammit. I called dibs on him long before you spotted him!* I had to do something fast, so I yelled across the room toward him.

"I'll take your order over here if you like, I'm not busy!" Everyone who wasn't paying any attention to me all night was now. They all watched the show I was putting on for them and smiled. Ruby, on the other hand, cursed me with her eyes. Whatever...

I cleared my throat and tried to sound cheerful without being overly enthusiastic about it.

"Well, hi there, what can I get you tonight?" I gave him my friendly smile as I spoke to his chest. *Chest? Eyes girl, look up at his eyes!*

He tensed his muscles ever so tightly which made his man nipples perk up just a tad bit. Have you ever wanted to suck a man's nipples so bad that your tongue hurt? God, mine did. *Get a hold of yourself, Charlese.*

"Um, what kind of beer do you have on tap?" He smiled. *Oh God, let me die right now in his arms, lap, anything that was part of him, please.*

"Ah, sir, no service if you're not wearing a shirt."

Wouldn't you know. Chester would start acting like he owned the place. Well, he did, but still!

I back slapped him on the chest with my hand and glared at him, smiling though.

"Chester, the man is hot," God is he ever, "and he just wants a drink, so what if he ain't got a shirt on. He's paying for the beer, so I don't know why you're reading him the rights and all."

Every guy there whooped and sang my praises loud.

"You tell him, Charlese!"

"Yeah, it's hot!"

"Chester, you jealous or something?" They all loved that one and started to laugh. Chester wasn't laughing.

"If I let him come in here not wearing a shirt, then I'd have to let everyone else and I ain't gonna do that, Charlese! Sorry sir, those are my rules." And he walked away.

"I guess I won't be having anything, sorry to have bothered you." He started to get up.

"No, wait!" I ran to the back of the restaurant and into the office. Chester always left a shirt here just in case he spilled something on himself and there it was. I grabbed it quick and came back over to him and handed him the shirt.

"Here, put this on and I'll get you your beer." Chalk one up for me!

"Charlese, what the hell you doing giving him my shirt?" Chester was madder than a hornet, but I didn't care.

"Because like I said, he was hot and thirsty, and I aim to please whoever walks through that door."

"Ok, what if Ernest walked through without a shirt on, would you do the same for him?" He smiled broadly now. He knew how I felt about Ernest; *everyone* knew how I felt about him. The man was smelly, fat, and had the biggest crush on me.

"I'd ... I'd still want him to stay." I tried to sound sincere, but it was hard, knowing how he looked and smelled. Garbage had better appeal.

"Oh, really? Ok, we'll just see about that. What does Mr. Gorgeous want to drink?" Smug, but I didn't care.

"He wants ... ah, I didn't ask."

"Good one, Charlese. Too busy looking at his chest; I'm surprised you knew how to find your way to the office."

I was bright red as I turned to go back to his table.

"Sorry, but I forgot to tell you the kind of beer we had." I rattled off the ten different taps we had, and he chose Coors.

"Say, are you doing anything after you close?"

Chester's shirt was too small for his enormous chest, so while he had it on, he didn't button it. All that muscle just gleamed up at me and I fixated on it with all my heart. I had to sigh.

"Charlese!"

I snapped out of my stupor to see what Chester wanted.

"What?"

"Beer?"

"You know I can't drink while working!" I treated Chester like he was being silly and snorted.

"I wasn't talking about you. What kind of beer does Mr. Gorgeous want or do I have to read his mind to find out?" Smugness was not becoming on Chester.

"Oh, he wants a Coors!" I tried to compose myself because I was not acting myself at all tonight.

"Thank you." He just shook his head.

"Well?" Mr. Gorgeous was speaking again. What was it about this guy who made everything around him disappear?

"Well, what?" I was in la la land now.

"Would you like to do something after you get off?"

"Oh, that! Um, sure! What'cha have in mind?" I sat across from him and just stared, not hearing Chester calling me to get my order.

"I thought we could, you know, go for a walk, talk a bit, maybe go to your place or mine?" His teeth were so white when he smiled, they reminded me of cottage cheese ... white and glistening.

All of a sudden, I heard this bell ringing to beat the band. Chester was trying to get my attention.

Everyone was laughing when I finally came out of my fog. "I'll be right back, don't go anywhere now, ya hear."

"I've been calling you to pick up your order, but you're so far gone that not even this stupid bell was getting through that thick fog you was sitting in! Wake up, Charlese, and wipe the drool off your face. Damn you're a sight tonight."

I looked at him and got all self-righteous. "I do not drool, that's sweat." I proceeded to dab my face with a napkin as I picked up the mug of beer.

"I can see the heat has made you hornier than a jack rabbit. Go sew your wild oats because I need a reliable worker tomorrow!"

"Thanks!"

I set the beer down, as well as myself, and said, "Let's get out of here. My boss is letting me off early." I gave him my *come-hither* look, and he chugged his beer down in seconds. I was astounded by that, I really was.

I went back into the office, got my purse, said my goodbyes to Chester, who just groaned his acknowledgement, and left.

"Oh, wait a second, you still have Chester's shirt on!"

"So I do." He turned to face me and slowly, very slowly, he slipped it off, expanding his chest as he did so, and I was *so* glad he did. My hands were itching to touch his tight muscles, not to mention other things. Whoa, slow down girl, this guy could very well be a mass murderer or something. I thought about that, and then snorted at the idea.

"What's so funny?" He looked himself over as if he had something on him that was making me laugh.

"Oh, it's nothing really."

"I'd like to hear, if you don't mind."

We had walked a bit, about a few blocks from the Chubby Wieners and came to the edge of the park and sat down on the bench by the pond. It was so peaceful. The moon shone on the stillness of the water and grasshoppers chirped their songs through the night air. It was a perfect setting.

"I was just thinking about ... oh I can't, you'd think I was nuttier than a fruitcake!"

"No, I won't. Go on, tell me." He got closer to me, and the smell of musk and earth filled my senses. This was a man, and I don't mean any man.

"Well, I was wondering just how tight your muscles were." Heat filled my face as a nice shade of red tinted my cheeks.

He turned slightly toward me and said, "Go ahead, touch all you want."

This was too good to be true! It was like Santa had just given me the best present ever, the kind that keeps giving and I was gonna take as much as I could. Slowly, with my hand shaking slightly, I touched his chest, warm, and lusciously tight. I prodded and poked, but in the most delicate way. He was like filet mignon, rare, oozing such juices and ... lord, he was stirring something powerful inside me. I was becoming ignited!

"Wow..." I said in hushed tones.

He laughed as his arms went around my waist, pulling me in toward him. Oh, oh, I think I just lit his fire as well!

"Your hands are so soft they're driving me wild." He leaned down and began to tease me with his lips.

They were full and very soft, and he did such magic with them. My neck was doing a little happy dance, not to mention other parts of me as well. I oozed in places I didn't know oozed, and I didn't want him to stop either. I moaned to his satisfaction.

"You like? I can tell, you smell ... ready."

What the hell did he mean by that, I smell *ready*? I started to sniff the air, but as far as I could tell I didn't smell anything but him, and I loved the way he smelled.

Before I knew it, he had my blouse unbuttoned and was kissing the swell between my breasts. I had just died and gone to heaven. I couldn't help but moan louder. *Oh, dear lord, don't stop.*

I never knew what love making could be until now. He was so masterful that every inch of my body was explored to its depths, and I explored his, and there was lots of him to explore and taste. I was like a kid in a candy store, tasting and savoring all sorts of flavors.

There was a slight pause in our togetherness. It had dawned on me that I didn't know his name and so I asked, "What's your name?" As I waited, I was straddling him, naked as a Jay Bird and loving every bit.

"Fred."

"Really? I would have guessed you to be a Robert or something exotic like ... Lazar." I kept my pace going. His eyes closed. He surely was enjoying himself, I could tell. That was until he whipped me onto my back and gave it all he had, and I just trembled with excitement. It was explosive and I was completely exhausted.

We lay there, in each other's arms, completely and wonderfully sated. Then he looked down at me, I mean really looked at me. I couldn't feel, see, or hear anything around us, it was like everything that didn't matter was gone and here we were. Then he spoke, softly, mesmerizing, seductively.

"Look to me and no other. Look to me when you thirst, when you hunger, for I will be the only one who will satisfy all your needs. Just like you have satisfied mine ... for all eternity."

Then, as if someone turned the volume on to the world, I was back.

"Did you say something?"

"No, but the sun will be up soon, and I must go. Get dressed."

I thought it funny he was so serious, and I had no idea why he worried about the sun, but I got dressed, and he took me home. Before he left me, he held me in his arms and inhaled. What was with him and my smell? Did I need to shower or something? He sniffed me so much that I swear he must be part dog or something.

"You smell intoxicating; I can't seem to get enough of you."

"Great, I guess that's a good thing then, huh? Well, I'll be seeing you around. Thanks for the great night!"

I turned out of his arms to unlock my door, but when I went to say goodbye, he was gone.

"Well, if that wasn't rude. I think I've just been used!" I went in, and as I shut the door, I noticed my neck ached on its side. I rubbed it but I felt nothing, just a slight pain. Odd.

7

RED APPLE CATACLYSM

"One summer, I was watching my nephew, Tommy. Nice boy, but you know how boys are ... wild! I, on the other hand, am not, and I had things to get done that were important. Like housework, but Tommy was being Tommy a bit too loud, and I was going to stop it."

The world shook all around me as I held on for dear life. Visions of my childhood played before my eyes. In flashes they came swooshing, one right after the other. I couldn't see. I was getting whipped in the face and knocked about my head. It was horrific, and I thought if I made it through this turmoil I would get down and strangle the life out of him.

"Stop shaking the tree branch, Tommy!"

Tommy was my nephew. As much as I loved him, there were times I wanted to strangle him. My sister, Candy, was a lenient parent and praised how wonderful her child was, that he never, ever got into any trouble. Damn, who put blinders on her, I wondered.

"I want lots of apples, Aunt Charlese, not just one!" His grubby little hands were still on the branch I was standing on, and it shook again.

"Thomas Andrew Chilton, if you don't stop shaking this branch, I'm gonna come down and shake you up, so stop it!" Dang if he wasn't a thorn in my backside today. Normally I wouldn't have him over, because I can only take so much, but my sister, God love her, had an OBGYN appointment and didn't have the nerve to take him along with her. I don't blame her one bit.

I jumped down and handed him an apple, to which he looked very sullen.

"Now what?" I bit into mine; it was juicy and sweet as could be.

"I wanted more than just one." He took his and looked at it as if it had cooties or something. Pitiful.

"Gran always told me that greed is to always want." Gran to me was the wisest person on earth.

"What's that supposed to mean?"

"It means like the apple I gave you or else and don't ask me what 'else' is, because you don't want to know." Then I gave him my serious face, which made him shiver. Good.

The rest of the day was somewhat quiet, Tommy played outside with a basketball I had in the garage, and I cleaned my house. It needed it badly, I mean *badly*. My living room especially needed a good, thorough clean. It wasn't a big room, simple in taste; a collection of mismatched furniture and knickknacks that spoke *home*. I liked this room a lot.

I was dusting when Tommy came running in.

"Aunt Charlese! Aunt Charlese!" He had a newspaper in his hand and his face was as white as a ghost.

"What's wrong Tommy?" He handed me the paper and on the front page, in big letters said, *Apocalypse.*

"Oh, Tommy, is that what you're afraid of, the end of the world?" I set it down on the coffee table and continued my dusting.

"But we should prepare for the end times, it's gonna be horrific and aren't you worried, Aunt Charlese?"

"Tommy, I ain't worried, because it ain't happening and neither should you, now scoot back outside and let me finish!" I swear, when I get married and have children ... then I stopped thinking, because the thought scared me.

Tommy, all beside himself, was royally miffed and so he set about preparing for when the world would truly end. Now, I had no idea what plans he was all set to do, but knowing what I do know of him, it couldn't be good.

"Tommy, don't you start anything ... you hear me?" I was hollering and dusting, multi-tasking they call it, and I was doing a fine job. It was a talent that I was blest with. Why, I remember one day when Gran was cleaning the house, I had gotten into a discussion with her. I don't remember exactly what it was about, but we were heavily into it, I know that much. Well, while we were discussing heavily, I had been in the bathroom, she in the living room and I was about to go out to sunbathe. Now, multi-tasking is tricky, like I said, so when I grabbed for my hair shiner, I didn't realize what I had actually grabbed. I sprayed a good amount in, like I always did, but it wasn't getting shiny, just drippy. So, I sprayed more, but it made it worse.

"Gran, what is wrong with this shine spray of mine? Come quick!"

Gran stopped what she was doing and came in. She looked at me and then got her glasses.

"Where's the eye-glass cleaner? I can't see a thing through them!" she said.

I handed her the bottle, and she sprayed her lenses good and started to rub. Well, when she put them on, everything looked foggy. She took them off and found they were all greasy-like and smeary. So, she sprayed again, meanwhile, there I stood with drippy hair looking like a drowned cat. She rubbed and rubbed, but it was worse than before!

"Lands sake, why aren't my glasses getting clean?" I took the bottle from her, read the label.

"Oh, good Lord, you've been using my shine spray on your glasses and ... *damn, I've been using your eye-glass cleaner on my hair!*" From then on, I *was* very careful to multi-task.

I was almost done with the house when I heard loud thumps hitting my roof top. It sounded like a hailstorm had sprouted up, but when I looked out the window, it was sunny. Then screams started in, loud and boisterous, several different levels of screams like there were a few dozen people outside in my yard. Thumps and then a big crash sounded behind me. There on the ground, a shiny red apple lay ... Tommy.

My blood began to boil. "If he wants an Apocalypse, he's gonna get one."

I took out the bottle of ketchup and smeared it all over me, ripped my shirt and pants and kicked off one shoe. Then, messed my hair up and ran outside screaming.

"The end of the world is here, save yourselves! Grab your children, your kin folk and get below." I grabbed Tommy; I ignored all the other kids and took him down to our tornado shelter. It was dark, dank, and small, perfect for my *end of the world* scenario. Tommy was dumbfounded, he had no idea I would react this way and so he started to believe my act. He chose the wrong person to trick; I took an acting class in college.

Now as it were, I used to play down here when I was little. This was my fort and it protected me from all the nasty boys who would tease me, so I had rigged up a few traps and noise makers. I looked at Tommy who was about to pee his pants and I looked at him real good.

"I can't save your mama, so I'm all you got now, ya hear? I will protect you till the day I die."

"A-Aunt Charlese, there ... there wasn't any real end of the world thing going on outside. I and ..."

"What you talking about, boy?" I grabbed his shirt collar and pulled him in close to my face and sneered at him with buggy eyes. It was a real good effect because I've never seen him so quiet. My voice was kinda craggy in tone which set the mood perfectly.

"I ... I don't know ..." His lip quivered and his little body shook like jello.

"Listen." I pretended like I heard something rustling above us. I waited a few seconds before I pulled a cord that was behind me, that was attached to some cans above us. When I thought the tension was just right, I pulled and pulled like a mad woman possessed. The cans rattled and made all kinds of noises. Tommy started to scream.

"Make it stop, please, I want to go home Aunt Charlese!" His hands went up over his ears and he shut his eyes tight.

"It's the end of the world, Tommy, I can't make it stop. We're destined to live our lives out with each other." Then I grabbed him and smothered him like gravy smothers mashed potatoes. It was a Kodak moment.

"No! It was me, Joey, Cleaver, and Jimmy. We made all that noise while you were in the house cleaning. Aunt

Charlese, you have to believe me!" He was pleading and I thought, God love him, he came out of his illness.

"I have a confession too, Tommy ..." And I proceeded to tell him.

Weeks had gone by since that fateful day. Tommy was over again, spending time with me and you know what, he was cleaning my living room real nice and doing a fine job.

8

BEACH PARTY ZOMBIE

"Have you ever watched those old beach movies with Annette Funicello and Frankie Avalon? Those were the best. One hot summer day, I had to get away from Dry Prong and go to the beach, but I think I got too much sun! Strange things began to happen."

It was one of those hot days, the kind where you don't want to do anything but lay around, and that's what I did, only on a beach. I had on my white bikini with the red polka dots, which looked really good next to my tan, and I was wearing my Foster Grants.

The beach was packed full of families, lovers walking hand in hand, and of course, those that love to play volleyball. It was a great day to be had by all, until ...

"Well, look what the lake washed up. I was wondering what smelled so bad." The voice was nasally, and becoming on annoying. Lydia Hankshaw.

. . .

I opened my eyes and got the shock of my life. Not only did Lydia have on a swimsuit, I'd say the swimsuit had Lydia. It was bright green, with netting that covered her cleavage, not by much though. It snugged in places that couldn't be snugged, which then jutted out other body parts. It was a mess, no doubt about that. She also wore one of those beach hats, with a wide brim and rainbow sunglasses. Look out Tara Banks, Lydia is on the runway!

"Why, good morning yourself," I said sweetly.

"I didn't say that!"

"I know, but that's the difference between you and me. I have class, you don't. Now, if you don't mind, you're blocking the sun." I was beaming from within. I finally told that bitch what for.

She took off with her big butt swaying in the sun. Whoever came up with the line, "Put it where the sun don't shine" got it all wrong, because the sun sure found itself on her behind.

After she had gone, I went back to sunbathing, while the noise of those having fun calmed my frazzled nerves. It's very rare for me to be here. I mean, I'm always working and when I'm not, I'm working at home. If you got time to lean, you got time to clean my Gran always told me.

An hour had gone by without a scuffle, and I was starting to get a bit warm. Sitting up, I noticed the water was mighty inviting. So, I got up and started to walk on down when I ended up running toward the water. The sand, from baking in the sun was so hot, my feet were burning! I ran right in, forget the inching in style, I needed cooling off in a big way!

Ah ... the cool water bathed my sore feet, and the deeper I got, the more refreshed I became. It was truly satisfying. I was now up to my waist when I sunk the rest of me under, it almost took my breath away, but boy oh boy, it was doing wonders for my soul. I just stayed there, my head the only visible part of me, and I watched while others were playing games, swimming with their inflatables, or just doing what I was doing ... people watching.

Just as I thought things couldn't be better, they weren't. A scream out of nowhere filled the air. Was someone drowning, was there a shark attack? *Shark attack ...*

"Excuse me, pardon me, excuse me ..." I wadded back to shore as fast as my little legs would carry me, but you can't move fast while in the water. It was like trying to run in a bog, and it's next to impossible to run in them things. I've tried it. Yup, Chester and I were hunting alligators with his Uncle Jimmy Nell when we caught one. It was 400 pounds and talk about your thrashing! It was twirling and twirling, and they had a terrible time with it. Well, I got up to get out of their way, when I tripped over the wire. I lost my balance and fell overboard! Man, you never saw anyone try to get back into that boat like I did. I felt like I was moving in slow motion. The thought of that alligator coming at me was enough to give me a heart attack. Anyway, I did make it back in and Chester, along with his uncle, killed it and ended up getting paid a mightily big sum.

Back to the screaming—

I got back to the shore just in time to see people scrambling all over the place, screaming and yelling to beat the band. It was like a wild animal was loose or something, and everyone was trying to get away from it — it wasn't an animal, but something was coming after people. It was a person, I think, but nobody ever looked like this one. He was tall, well built, ugly as sin, and smelled just as bad, if sin had an odor. His swimming trucks were not altogether there. Parts of him were hanging out and I must admit, he did have something worth smiling about. What was wrong with me? Here I am, watching a true-life Zombie Apocalypse right before my very eyes, and I'm getting heated over some stinking guy's junk. Where are my scruples?

As I stood, motionless, I hadn't noticed that Zombie 'Moon Doggie' had spotted me and decided to make my acquaintance. That was my exit cue, so I took off, but again, have you ever tried to run in the sand, fast? And did you know that Zombies could run fast? All the Zombies I ever saw, walked like they had dookie in their pants, but not my Moon Doggie, his were ... enough. I tried as best as I could, but it wasn't enough. Next thing I knew he had grabbed hold of my — bikini bottom, that's when I stopped. No way, no how was I gonna keep on running only to have my panties torn off of me. Seeing how his were almost off, I didn't want to give him any ideas.

What do you say to a Zombie, other than scream? So, I swatted his hand. "Get your damn hand off my swimsuit. *Bottom* just didn't sound right, again, didn't want to give him any ideas. He just gave me that dead stare, but he drooled. Charming ain't he? "I said get your hand off my swimsuit, now!" He then smiled.

When he opened his mouth to speak, I swore a fly came out. Now, that's just gross.

He coughed, didn't know they could, and said, "Annette?"

Did I hear him correctly, or did he just call me Annette? "I beg your pardon?"

"A-Annette?" And pulled me in closer.

I thought so. "Hunny, I ain't your Funicello, my name is Charlese." *Why* am I introducing myself?

"No, you Annette, come ..."

I almost got him loose when behind him came a group of other charming fellows. All of them beefed up to the max, not a one looked like the zombies I've seen on TV. These were masculine, beefy guys, hunkered up for battle and like my Moon Doggie, half dressed.

"Uh, you've got company." I motioned for him to look, which he did, but then looked at me with fear. I had to ask myself this, but why would anyone be afraid of his own kind?

"Trouble!" was all he said.

"Yeah, I know, why are you telling me that? Aren't they your buds?" Damn, if I'm not dealing with a two-year-old.

"No! We fight! My girl!" Then started to drag me toward them.

Then it hit me, Blanket Beach Bingo, are these zombies reenacting the 1965 movie? I've got to be having a nightmare. Must have been that Fish Taco I ate last night, looked good, but tasted like it should have stayed in the ocean.

"Stop. Stop! Stop! I ain't fighting no zombies and I sure ain't your girl either. God ... or whoever may have endowed you handsomely, but that don't mean I love you. Besides, this ain't a movie that's going on here, more like a nightmare if you ask me! I don't know where you guys came from, but I'm leaving and take your stinking hands off me!" I jerked my hand out of his so forcefully his own hand came off. I screamed.

"Sugar! Come back!"

I just kept on running all the way back to my blanket, got my stuff, and headed for my car. As the engine came to life, I noticed all the zombie guys waving at me. This is *so* weird! I waved back as I hightailed it out of the parking lot.

A mile down the road, I felt better, but not completely. It was a nightmare. I never, ever dreamed that something like that could ever happen, on TV yes, real life, no. I needed some noise to take my mind off what had just happened. When I switched on my radio the song, <u>These Are the Good Times</u>, by Frankie Avalon came on ... it was from the movie Beach Party Bingo — déjà vu.

9

LOVE ON THE FLY

"Well, with the summer, we do get some rain and this time it poured cats and ... geese. Yeah, another, yet funny story about Willodean and her guest. Sit down and take a load off, this will take some time telling."

It was another crap day in Dry Prong, and I was fit to be tied. For days on end the weather had been gloomy, gray, and wet. Rain kept on coming and not letting up at all and I swore I thought I saw someone pull out their canoe.

I looked over at Willodean Ferris' house and so far, it hadn't budged off its foundation, not yet that is, but her yard was beginning to look like a pond or so the geese thought so, for there were three of them gliding along the water. I decided to give her a call.

"Hey Willodean, how are you holding up?"

"Oh, I guess alright, but you know, I'm really worried about something?" Her voice got all shaky when she spoke.

"What's troubling you?" Now, if you know Willodean like I do, then you know a bug could have smiled at her and she'd be having a fit.

"Well, the geese seemed to have found a home in my backyard and ... well, what's gonna happen when the water dries up?"

See, I told you so. "I guess they'll just fly away to some other pond. Is that a problem?"

"Well, yeah, that's a problem because we're like family now. I mean, look how content they are back there! I wouldn't want them to leave, thinking I took their water away from them. I don't like hurting anybody you know that, even if they are just animals."

I stood there for a moment, let what she just said sink in real deep and then spoke, "Hunny, I don't think those geese could care less whether you had water or not, because they're just geese! They go wherever they find water and park themselves in it. They don't know whose lawn or park it is, they just come!"

"Oh, Charlese, now you don't mean that really do you? They certainly do know where they're at. They know it's me, because I always leave breadcrumbs out for them to eat on the old tree stump."

"Willodean, unless you have a sign that says, The Honkers Bread Tray Café, they really don't know. To them it's food left outside, nothing else."

There was silence for a few seconds, I could hear her breathing, sniffling ... sniffling?

"Willodean, are you crying?"

"No, I mean, yes. They can't leave me! Charlese will you help me make a fence around my pond so that they won't fly away?"

I was afraid of this, I surely was. I could see it coming just as plain as the nose on my face and it did, big time. I wanted to tell her that putting up that stupid fence wasn't going to keep them ... they can fly for pity's sake! As for the *pond*, it wasn't going to stay either, because there was never a pond to begin with, it's just over-soaked ground. Pond my fat brother's ass. Tension was building up inside me.

"Are you serious? Willodean, they can fly, they have wings and all. Putting up that fence ..."

"Don't you tell me another negative thought Charlese, you're gonna help me like a friend should and that's all there is to it. Now, you coming to help me or are you gonna be impolite?"

She just trumped me, the impolite card. My gran always told me to be polite, to be neighborly, because what you give to those in need you reap big rewards. I like to know what my big reward was gonna be putting up that fence. I would also like to know where Gran learned that from, because whoever said it didn't know Willodean very well.

"Oh, alright I'll be over." I slammed the phone down on its receiver and swore a bunch of times as I stomped into my bedroom to get my work clothes.

Willodean has done some dumb things in her life, but I would have to say that this beat them all. I was testy, tugging at my clothes as I changed and shoved my feet into my crummy old tennis shoes. I was so mad I wanted to just throw my shoes instead. I wanted to throw them at something or someone, Willodean perhaps. The thought made me smile. "No, I can't do that."

Then I stomped my way over to her house. She stood there cooing at the dumb geese and talking all sugary to them. Made my stomach turn it did. I cleared my throat to get her attention.

"Oh, you've come to help me. How thoughtful!" She smiled

so big that her teeth and gums took up most of her face. Charming.

"Yeah ... thoughtful. What do you want me to do?" I so did not want to be here. No, no, no!

"Well, see that chicken wire and those metal fence thingies, we need to put the fence thingies in the ground, space them about three feet apart in a nice circle, then we'll wrap the chicken wire around them!"

I didn't say anything, because if I had, well, you don't want to know. I went over, took one of the green, metal *thingies,* and began to shove them into the ground. Good thing the ground was soaked because it just made working easier and faster. There is a God. As soon as I got all the posts in, I looked for Willodean to see if she was ready for the chicken wire ... she was. I just drooped my head in disbelief. There she was, draped with a chef's apron, long, long, green cleaning gloves and goggles. Oh, and shower cap. Her hands held up in front of her as if she were about to operate.

"What in blue blazes are you dressed up like that for?" I felt the pangs of laughter creeping up, and I slapped my hand over my mouth when it kicked in.

With the look of sheer seriousness she said, "Why Charlese, when you're working with wire you should always be safe."

That's when I let it rip. "Safe? Safe from what?"

She straightened herself up taller and glared at me. "Why safe from getting hurt by the wire of course!"

I sniggered. "Ok, Willodean, whatever. Let's just get this done so I can enjoy the rest of my day."

The drizzle of rain that had been falling just kept on, and I was becoming cold and terse. There I was, holding the roll of chicken wire as *Go Go Gadget* hooked the wire around the posts. It looked dreadful, but Willodean thought it was a work of art. I was just glad to be finished.

"There, see? Doesn't it look lovely? And my geese will always be here to greet me! I could sit out here and share my lunch with them and watch them swim. Thank you, Charlese, for helping me."

Seeing her face all lit up like a candle and hearing how thrilled she was at having them geese in her yard, well, I was happy for her. "Glad to have helped. I'm going now, take care."

I slowly turned myself around and headed home.

The days of doom and gloom finally left, and I woke to find sunshine coming through my windows. It was going to be a great day.

"Come back, come back don't leave, look I have breadcrumbs!"

I didn't have to look. I already knew what had happened. The geese were leaving, just like I told her.

"Stupid birds!"

"Geese ... "I mumbled to myself.

10

SHREDDED WHEAT CATASTROPHE

"Remember the story on the beach? With the zombies and all, well, it happened again. Damn, if they don't beat all! Who'd of thought that Dry Prong would be a popular place for the undead to hang out. Well, this here is a long one, so you best sit down if you haven't yet."

Dry Prong was having its usual dry season, where everything and everyone screamed for water. Just this morning, I looked at my front lawn and heaved a heavy sigh.

"Shredded wheat." That's what my lawn looked like. All I needed was a little milk and my breakfast would be complete.

"Hey, Charlese! Whatcha looking at?"

Billy Beauford had just walked up and caught me staring at what once was a beautiful, green lawn. "Oh, hey yourself, what brings you out this way?"

Now I've known Billy since I was knee high to a grasshopper and even then, I didn't like him much, but now that I've grown up, I don't kick him in the shins anymore, I've resisted those temptations.

"I was on my way to the Five and Dime to get me a Coke. You want to come along?"

"Why sure, just you mind yourself though. I'm hot and cantankerous, a force you do not want to mess with." I was too. Gran, if she was still around, would stay clear away from me when I was in such a mood.

"Oh, no, no, no … "and held the last *no* out for a few seconds longer before stopping.

I eyed him curiously, "We'll just see about that." I was cautious, but decided to go anyway, besides, the thought of an icy, cold drink sounded real good.

The Five and Dime was a mile down the road and by the time we got there sweat was trickling down my back. I looked over at Billy and he looked as though he had just finished running a race. His T-shirt was drenched, and his face was beet red.

As I came up to the door, Billy ran in front and opened it for me. "After you." He said, and swept his arm toward the opening, a gesture of gentlemanly ways, I wasn't having any of it. If I had known any better, which I do, he was up to something. I eyed him curiously.

"What?" he questioned.

"You know what; I know what you're up to, so you can just get them thoughts out of your head."

"Charlese, I wouldn't …"

Again, I said nothing but gave him my look of death. He shut his mouth real quick like.

Now the Five and Dime store is not one I frequent a lot, but when I do, it's usually for their sale items that I may need from time to time. Making my way toward the back of the store, I noticed how eerily quiet and still it was. I looked over at the owner who always stood behind the front counter. He seemed to be ok, but as I stared longer, I noticed he hadn't flinched or moved a muscle. Odd. That's when I turned back around and went to the counter.

"Mr. Zamood? Um, you okay?" I waved my hand in front of his face ... nothing. He was so still, like a wooden duck floating on a pond.

I went hesitantly about my business, looking over at Mr. Zamood every once in a while, when I came face to face with a drink.

"Here you go, Charlese! I went ahead and got you a drink. Hope you like it. It's Coke." He was grinning from ear to ear and so pleased with himself.

Slightly startled, I replied politely, "Why thank you Billy, that was real nice of you." I sparkled and oozed excitement, which made his day.

We went over to the counter where Mr. Zamood stood stock still. Billy, not realizing what was going on, was jabbering away, and fishing his money out of his pocket while complaining how hot the weather was.

"Billy?"

"Yeah?"

"I think something is wrong with Mr. Zamood, see." I pointed, hoping he'd see what I was talking about, and he did. Next thing I knew Billy was waving his hand and making faces at the man. Really?

"Billy, even though Mr. Zamood ... "

Then the strangest thing happened, Mr. Zamood started to foam at the mouth and his eyes rolled back into his head. He was convulsing!

"Billy, get away!" But it was too late. Mr. Zamood grabbed hold of Billy's throat and pulled him inward.

Protection mode set in, and I grabbed his ankles and held

on for dear life. There we were, having ourselves a human tug-of-war and as far as I could see Mr. Zamood was winning.

"You let go of him you hear me?" I placed my feet against the bottom of the front counter, using it as leverage, but for some strange reason, Mr. Zamood was extremely strong, especially for being sixty-nine years old. Nothing I said to him got through. He was bound and determined to have Billy for himself and on any given day I'd say go for it, but his was different, Billy was in danger.

I looked around desperately for anything I could use as a weapon and the only thing I spotted was a stand for Zippo Lighters. Now, for a few seconds the thought of zombies came to mind, and I remember watching a TV show that had burning zombies in a road. Mr. Zamood didn't seem like a zombie normally, but today he had all the signs of being just that. I took a deep breath. I realized I had to kill a man. I was not going to make Gran happy, that's for sure.

The trick now was how to get one of them lighters without losing Billy in the process. I was only inches away, so if I let go for just a second, not much would happen, hopefully.

"Sorry, Billy, but I have to do this, you'll thank me in the end!"

"What?"

I let go with my left hand and off he went over the counter. I quickly grabbed me a shiny, red lighter, flicked open the lid, and clicked the lever which would ignite the gas with a spark. All this time, Billy was battling a life and death situation, and it wasn't looking too good either.

"Alright you, I warned you and now you're toast!" I reached over the counter and lit the corner of Mr. Zamood's shirt. It caught fire real fast, and the flames spread up and outward as his whole shirt was now on fire. He started to scream and bat at the flames, while I yelled at Billy to run.

"Come on, Billy, let's get out of here quick!"

I waited as he climbed over the counter and out we went. We ran until our legs couldn't run no more and then sank to the ground with exhaustion. I had never in my life been so afraid.

"You ok?" I said, panting like a dog in summer. My throat was even more parched than when we first started out.

We sat there for a while. Sirens coming from a distance got louder and louder as black smoke streamed up into the sky. Billy just pointed as he gasped for a breath. I didn't even want to imagine what was going on now, but I had a pretty good idea. Not only was Mr. Zamood on fire, but the store too. Oh, boy.

"What do you suppose Mr. Zamood was?" Billy sounded breathy.

I hadn't a clue. Mr. Zamood wasn't from these parts, he was from India, and if their culture had a tendency for zombies then I guess that's what he was, but I couldn't be sure. I knew though that we'd never know the real answer, dead people don't talk or so I've been told.

"Know what Billy? You owe me a Coke, but seeing how I'm feeling generous, how about you coming over and I'll give you one?"

Billy smiled like I've never seen him smile before. "You sure?"

"Yes, I'm sure, but mind you, this ain't no invitation for catching some bases. You just mind your p's and q's or else!"

"Oh, sure, sure, I'll behave, besides, you saved my life, I ain't gonna ruin that for nothing. So, um, thank you."

We were only minutes away from my house and by the time we had reached my front porch I told him to have a seat and I'd be right back. I went into the kitchen and opened the cabinet. I decided to use my bright, orange tumblers that Gran had gotten from Woolworths a long time ago. They always made me feel special, and today I *was* feeling special. I had just saved a person's life and to me, that was a big deal.

Just as I was pouring two hands wrapped themselves around my waist. I hadn't heard Billy come in.

"Charlese, I just want you to know, just how appreciative I am by the way you saved my life today. That was a brave thing you did today." He snuggled in closer, and I got the rare feeling that he was overly grateful in more ways than one.

"Billy, if you don't let go of me this instant, I'll show you the meaning of the word *appreciate* real fast." But my words went on deaf ears as lips nuzzled my neck.

Two can play this game.

I brought my arms up, in a gesture that gave the impression that I was allowing him to take pleasure in me and then, without a flinch from me, grabbed a handful of hair in both hands and pulled.

"Oh, Charlese, let go, let go! You're hurting me!" His hands reached up to grab mine, but I let him have it below and kicked him in the shins. He was *owing* and *ooing* as legs were going up and down, trying to move away my feet.

"Why should I? You weasel you! How dare you take liberties on me after what I did! Are you insane?" I held on fast, I wasn't letting this one go, not yet at least.

"I'm sorry, just let go!" Sorry my ass.

"If I let go, you promise to walk out that door and never, and I *mean* never come back to my house again?" He squirmed and thought about that for a second.

"I promise, just let go!"

I held on for a little bit longer. I was enjoying seeing him squirm like a worm on a hook, but I knew I had to let him go, so I did and backed away.

"Out!" I said and pointed to the direction of my door. He rubbed his head all the while looking like a bad puppy with his tail between his legs ... come to think of it, you could probably take that literally. He moseyed past me and out the door, the whole time rubbing his damn head. I watched him go down the steps off my porch, across the yard to the street and back to his house. Good.

Just before I went in to clean up, I looked at my lawn and sighed.

11

WINTER'S RALLY

"To cool things down a bit, I have yet another tale to be told. It's about winter. Yes, believe it or not we get snow. Not a lot, though if you were to ask anyone around her how the winters are, they'd tell horrific stories. Truly! Let me tell you one of my stories."

Winter came, and with it, a beautiful blanket of snow covered the ground. Dry Prong was a winter wonderland and as usual, everything was closed. We got a whopping one inch.

Weathermen on the television and radio sent out their advisories: NO ONE WAS TO GO OUT UNLESS ABSOLUTELY NECESSARY.

So, there I was, standing by my bay window, watching dumb people attempt to go somewhere. You'd think that we had a foot of snow or something! It was better than watching the T.V. I got my cup of coffee and toast, pulled up a chair, and watched.

Now, Mr. O'Shay who lives two houses down from me was swearing up a storm because his snowblower kept jamming up ... on an inch of snow. Damn, where'd he get that blower anyway? Florida?

Then, there were the Sullivans. They lived across the street and were the most intelligent people I've ever met. Level-headed ... today though, not so much. I didn't know we had Arctic winds and temperatures setting in, but looking at Mr. Sullivan, AKA Igloo man, we were. Mrs. Igloo, also dressed in the thickest of outer wear, was sporting snowshoes, of all things. Guess she didn't want to sink into the cement driveway.

They both waved at me. I lifted my coffee cup to them and smiled. Mrs. Igloo toppled over just then. The Arctic winds must have overpowered her, or most likely the snowshoes.

As I sat, laughing and enjoying the sights before me a car going about 5 miles per hour stopped ... Willodean.

"Oh, good Lord! Is she nuts?" Paused for thought ... yes. "What is she doing out there? She has a bad enough time as it is walking in flip-flops!

I sat on the edge of my chair, waiting for that fearful cry ...

"Charlese!"

... And we have lift off.

I didn't run. Willodean would be there even if three days had gone by. I put my boots on, winter coat, and made my way through the mighty blizzard. Blizzard my foot, dogs were outside running around like it was summer.

"What now, Willodean?"

"What? I can't hear you in this windstorm!" she yelled.

I just looked at her.

"You got your heater fan turned on high! Turn it off. There, can you hear me now?"

"Why, yes! Charlese, I'm stuck, can you help?"

She was stuck. In an inch of snow.

"In what?" I asked.

"In what? IN WHAT?"

Damn if this ain't gonna take all day. So, I spoke ever so slowly, enunciating each word carefully so that she would understand me.

"What. Are. You. Stuck. In?" I wanted to add in dumbass, but that wouldn't be polite.

"Snow! I'm stuck in the snow, Charlese!"

"Willodean, I've been in Chicago in the wintertime. This …" and I motioned with my arms, "This is nothing compared to what they have. Just give your car a **little** gas, turn your wheel to the left and pull into your driveway."

I stepped away. Far away and watched as she **gunned** it. So much for giving it a little gas. Snow, dirt, and rock spit out the rear end, as a cloud of smoke filled the air. It was like watching the start of a drag race, though she wasn't going anywhere fast. Safe to say she wouldn't be stuck anymore, because the snow under the tires melted from the extreme heat.

"Willodean! Stop! STOP!"

She rolled down her window, "I told you I was stuck! Oh, Lord, how am I ever gonna get home?"

I looked over at her house which was 20 feet away, her driveway, 2 feet away, then said, "Walk it."

She looked at me like I had smoke coming out of my ears.

"Walk it? Walk it? Are you crazy? My car is stuck, and you want me to walk and get stuck myself?"

Then, I noticed something. Something that made my patience evaporate like the snow did under her tires.

"Willodean, is your car in park?"

"Yes, I always put it in park when I stop."

"Did ya think to put it … get out … GET OUT!"

She got out and I got in. I placed the car in DRIVE. Now, she has these little ravines on either side of her driveway for excess rainwater, yeah ... that's where I drove her car into. She screamed like a banshee.

"Charlese, have you gone mad? Are you insane?"

I got out. Shut the door.

"Nope. I just made you really stuck."

12

SANTA'S GOT A BRAND-NEW BAG

"I don't know how to begin with this next story. It is not a good story, in that someone dies. Someone who we have all loved since childhood. So, if you have any kids around, tell them to go away or watch the television. They will be traumatized for life."

Snow falling outside, like bits of fluff, thick and fat. Children throwing snowballs with screams of delight. Horses off in the distance looking so regal as puffs of steam emitted from their nostrils. So peaceful...

"Damn this tree!"

...and so, it begins.

"Willodean, what's wrong now?" I was so exasperated with her.

"It has no good side."

Oh, here we go again. "Good side?"

"Yes, Charlese. Everything and everybody has a good side, and this tree has no good side whatsoever."

"Oh, sweet Jesus, just put the tree up and decorate the damn thing. This is supposed to be fun, so...have fun!"

I left her to do her business and got myself a soothing cup of coffee, the elixir of life.

I started to pour the rich, dark brown...ooze? The blood began to boil as my cheeks turned a nice, bright scarlet red.

"Willodean!"

She came in. Lights entangled her body with tinsel in her hair. "What..." in a low register of disgust.

"What or better yet, how did you make the coffee?"

Her eyes lit up like a Christmas tree and said, "Oh, I thought I'd make something special for today."

"You mean 'mud'..."

"No, not mud, latte'"

"...Latte'?" I poured her a cup of glop. It came out of the pot thick and brown and oozing with pure disgust.

"Yeah, latte'!" She beamed.

I just stood there, mouth gaping wide, then I shook it at her.

"This is not latte. This is crap in a cup!"

A tear started to run down her cheek, and I knew I had gone too far.

"Willodean, I'm sorry, it's just that I had a bad night and that doesn't excuse me, but I'm a tad on the bitchy side."

"Ya think?" Then she walked out, tinsel trailing behind her, and continued her decorating.

I have to say, she's a true friend. Most would have walked out, but not Willodean.

After fifteen minutes of cleaning my pot, I had fresh coffee brewing and the smell put a smile on my face...I finally thought my day was not totally ruined, but I spoke too soon.

I don't remember how long I was in the kitchen, but I

thought it had been too quiet in the living room. Putting my cup in the sink, I went in to check.

"Willodean?" The room was empty. Damn I really did it now, she left and it's my fault.

I quickly changed my clothes and put on my Arizona jeans and big woolen sweater. I was heading for the great outdoors... then a thought entered my head. I should call, see if she got home alright before coming over. Being upset as she was, she may not want to see me at all.

I picked the receiver up, punched in her number...one ring, two rings...three rings...then her answering machine came on...

"Hi! Y'all reached the Ferris residence, but I can't come to the phone. Please leave a message and I'll call ya right back when I can!"

Now normally if someone wasn't home, I wouldn't worry, but I was worrying.

"Where could she have gone too?" I wondered out loud.

Scanning the area, I didn't see anything out of place, except for a pine tree that was decorated for Christmas and something squirming around half out of their mind...

"Willodean!"

I ran as fast as my legs could carry me, and the closer I got, the more horrific Willodean looked. She was a tangled mess of branches, sap, lights, and her hair looked like she had stuck her finger in a light socket.

"Oh, Willodean, what has happened to you?" I tried to untangle her, but with great difficulty. Just when I thought I got the gist of the sordid mess, the more it got knotted. It wasn't until after much screaming and swearing that I finally got her out of her mess. I wasn't the one screaming Willodean was. I was the one swearing.

"S-some nut job must have thought I was a Christmas ornament and tried to hang me, but I was victorious!" The poor girl was serious. How she thought she was victorious I have no idea, but she was glowing with pride that much I could tell.

"Ah, hunny, how you think you was victorious and all, because you were in a tree looking like a sock with static."

Willodean organized herself and proudly said, "Look under the tree and see for yourself!"

I was a bit leery as to what I'd find, but I did as she asked and got the shock of my life. There on the ground was...Santa! He was all in his glory, red suit with gold buttons, black leather boots, the whitest beard I have ever seen, and the creepiest eyes that were wide open with fright.

"Willodean, do you know who that is?" I was astounded.

"Of course I do. That's Santa Claus!"

"He's a human tree stand! I mean, how did you ever manage to shove the butt end of this here tree into his mouth?" I quickly stopped her from telling me all the gory details. Christmas will never be the same again...Christmas will never be ever!

"I put it there myself..." She was so proud of herself.

I looked at her incredulously. "But..."

"Oh that, yeah well, you see after I used him as my tree stand, I thought I should decorate it, you know, to draw people's attention away from seeing him."

I must have still looked puzzled because she continued.

"Isn't it obvious?" Willodean is not the best at explanations. It literally takes her several tries before she gets it right...God love her.

"Not really...you still..."

She huffed, took a deep breath, and began again.

"While decorating, I got snagged by a branch and then when I had that all fixed, the lights got all funky, so I was trying to fix them, but I guess I just made things worse."

"But you killed Father Christmas, you know...Santa Claus

the man who goes around giving gifts to all good girls and boys?" I was so confused my head hurt.

She paused, then kept silent. I could tell the wheels were whirling around in that empty head of hers and then they too got all tangled.

"Never mind explaining, it's too painful watching you try to tell me." It really was. I felt her pain, I literally did. My head was aching, and all I wanted to do is get back home and hoped that all this was truly a bad nightmare.

Later that night, as the stars filled the sky, I sat on my couch, bundled in my Gran's Afghan and stared at my Christmas tree. Chester came in—it was our date night—and sat next to me.

"Charlese, why does your tree look like it's giving birth to a string of lights?" His head was tilted to one side.

I just smiled at his big ole face and told him that Willodean had done my tree...that's all that was needed to be said and it was.

"Well, that about does it for now. I sure hope you enjoyed our stories about Dry Prong and its citizens. Share this book with your friends and give them a laugh or two. Well, ya'll come back now ya hear?"

ABOUT THE AUTHOR

Sue Mydliak has been writing for 11 years now. She got her first start in the publishing world with her Flash Fiction, The Clearing, which appeared in Issue 7 of Mississippi Crow magazine. From there she has had numerous publications. She is currently working on the final book in her Rosewood series which she hopes to have finished by October.

She lives in Illinois with her family and works as a Special Education Paraprofessional at the local High School and has held this position for 14+ years.

To learn more about Sue Mydliak and discover more Next Chapter authors, visit our website at www.nextchapter.pub.